Charley's First Night

For Ken, who knows a LOT about first nights ~A. H.

For Finn and Niamh ~H. O.

Text copyright © 2012 by Amy Hest
Illustrations copyright © 2012 by Helen Oxenbury

First edition 2012

Library of Congress Cataloging-in-Publication Data is available.
Library of Congress Catalog Card Number pending
ISBN 978-0-7636-4055-2

12 13 14 15 16 17 SCP 10 9 8 7 6 5 4 3 2 1

Printed in Humen, Dongguan, China

This book was typeset in Aged.
The illustrations were done in pencil and watercolor.

Candlewick Press
99 Dover Street
Somerville, Massachusetts 02144

visit us at www.candlewick.com

Charley's First Night

Amy Hest

illustrated by Helen Oxenbury

CANDLEWICK PRESS

It was snowing that night,
and Charley wanted me
to carry him home.

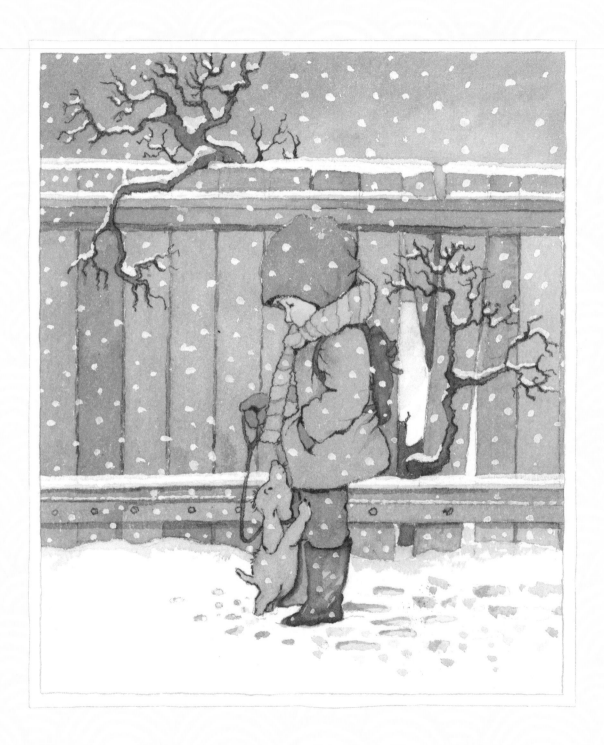

So I carried him all the way home.

I carried him in my old baby blanket,
which was soft and midnight blue, and we
were new together and I was very, very careful
not to slip in the snow and I thought about
his name. I was the one who thought up
his name. Charley. Charley Korn.
My name is Henry.
Henry Korn.

"This is home." That's what I told Charley when we got home, and I showed him all the rooms, including my room.

I showed him my bed and the place where my mother hides your birthday present when it's the day before your birthday. "This is home, Charley." I said that a lot so Charley would know he was home.

My mother (Mrs. Korn) and my father (Mr. Korn) were pretty clear about who would be in charge of walking Charley. *(I would be in charge of walking Charley, they said, and I couldn't wait to walk Charley every day forever.)* They were pretty clear about who would be in charge of feeding Charley. *(I would be in charge of feeding Charley, they said, and I couldn't wait to feed Charley every day forever.)*

They were also pretty clear about where Charley would be sleeping. (*Charley would be sleeping in the kitchen, they said, and I thought about Charley in the kitchen, alone every night forever.*)

"Charley wants to sleep in my room," I said.

"Charley will be sleeping in the kitchen," they said.

We fixed up a pillow-bed for Charley in the kitchen, under the table where the heat comes up, and I put my old bear, Bobo, in the pillow-bed for Charley and I thought about how I used to sleep with Bobo every night. I put my small red clock between Charley and Bobo —*tick-tock-tick-tock*— like another little heartbeat in the night.

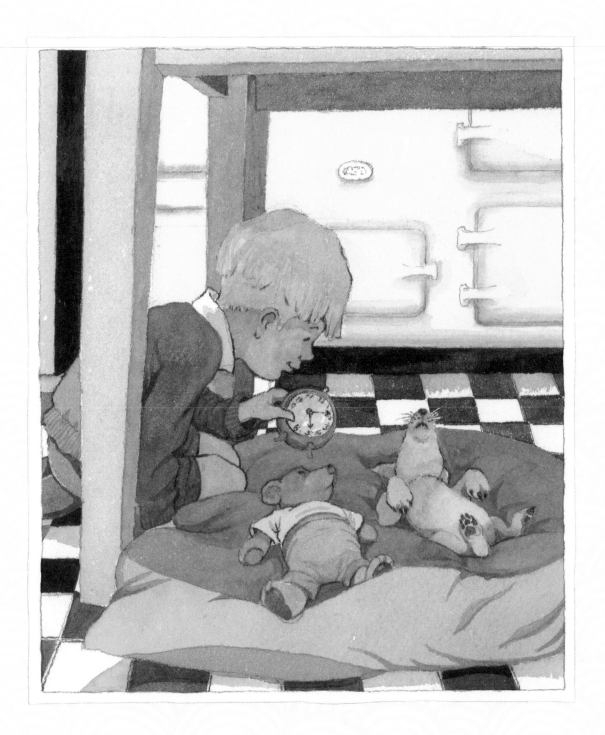

Charley curled up in a ball and I put my
face next to his and I waited for Charley
to fall asleep, and I thought about how my
mother and father sometimes used to wait for
me to fall asleep and soon Charley fell asleep.
He made a soft breathing sound and his soft
breathing sound made me sleepy, too.

I went to my room and sat up in my bed and looked out the window and snow was falling, over the city and the park and the trees in the park, and I thought about playing with Charley in the park in the snow.

The crying started in
the middle of the night
and you knew right away
it was Charley.

"Don't cry, Charley! Don't cry!" I ran to
the kitchen and scooped him and held him
close in my strong arms, and he shivered.

Slowly we walked around the house and I
showed him my room again and my bed.
I showed him my mother
and father, sound asleep
in their bed, and held
Charley close in my
strong arms.

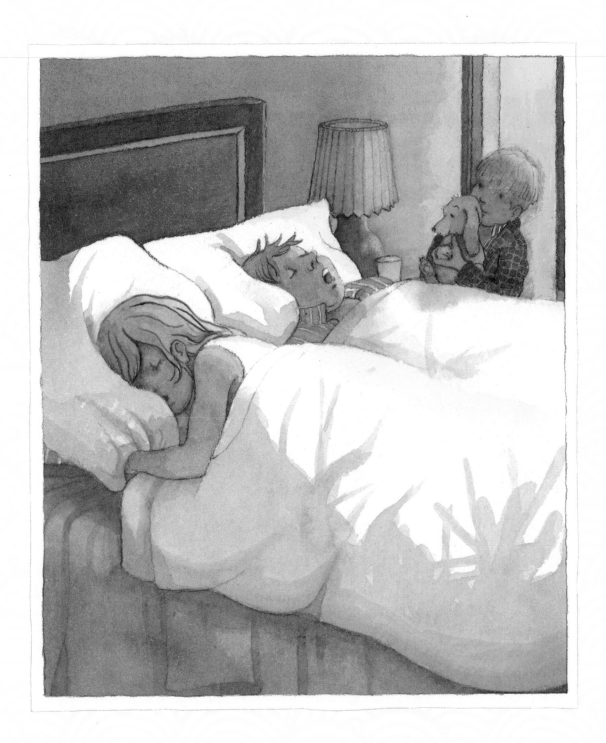

After a while I put Charley in his pillow-bed and rubbed his tummy and Charley smiled the way a friend smiles when you say "Hey, let's be friends forever!" I rubbed his back and the soft place behind his ears and he was really, really sleepy and the moon made its own light that night in the kitchen, right near Charley.

"'Night, Charley," I said.

"'Night, Charley boy."

A long time later, I heard crying again and I flew out of bed to Charley.

"Don't cry, Charley! Don't cry!" I scooped him up and held him close in my strong arms and he shivered. I showed him how the moon made its own light in the kitchen that night. "The moon did it for you," I told Charley, and he licked my nose and it tickled.

Slowly we walked
around the house
again and I showed him
my room again. Charley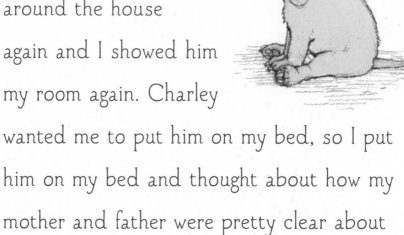
wanted me to put him on my bed, so I put
him on my bed and thought about how my
mother and father were pretty clear about
where Charley should not sleep.

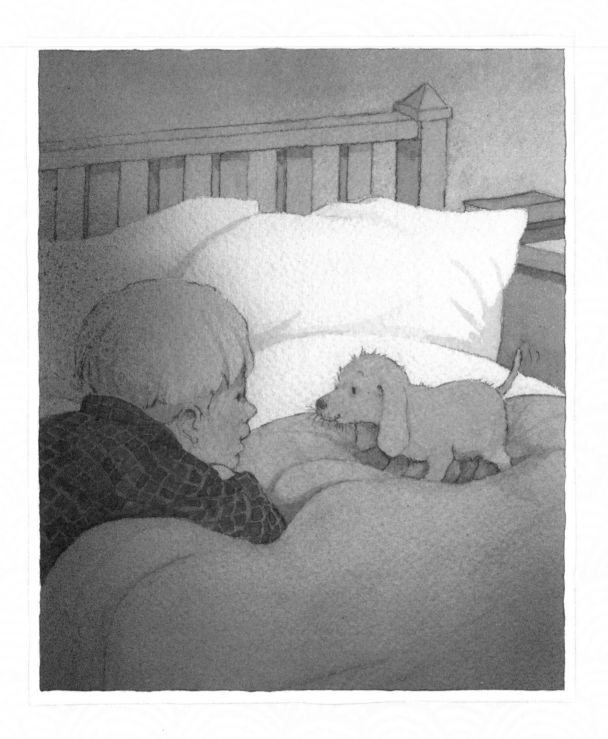

Charley wanted me on my bed, so I lay down on the bed next to Charley and we looked in each other's eyes. Charley has brown eyes and mine are green and I told him we could be best friends if he wants and Charley looked in my eyes and I looked in his. "I love you, Charley boy." That's what I told Charley.

We didn't mean to fall asleep, but we both fell asleep on my bed . . .

and that's exactly where we slept all through
the night on Charley's first night.